PUFFIN BOOKS

Marmalade Atkins in Space

Andrew Davies is a well-known and successful writer for film, television and the stage. He has written numerous children's books, including *Conrad's War*, which won the *Guardian* Children's Award in 1978, as well as a number of books for adults. He wrote the original highly acclaimed television series of *Marmalade Atkins*, which was broadcast by Thames in 1982. Andrew has two grown-up children and lives in Kenilworth, where the *Marmalade Atkins'* books are set.

Also by Andrew Davies

MARMALADE ATKINS' DREADFUL DEEDS

Marmalade Atkins
in Space

Andrew Davies

Illustrations by
John Laing

PUFFIN BOOKS

PUFFIN BOOKS

Published by the Penguin Group
Penguin Books Ltd, 27 Wrights Lane, London W8 5TZ, England
Penguin Books USA Inc., 375 Hudson Street, New York, New York 10014, USA
Penguin Books Australia Ltd, Ringwood, Victoria, Australia
Penguin Books Canada Ltd, 10 Alcorn Avenue, Toronto, Ontario, Canada M4V 3B2
Penguin Books (NZ) Ltd, 182–190 Wairau Road, Auckland 10, New Zealand

Penguin Books Ltd, Registered Offices: Harmondsworth, Middlesex, England

First published by Abelard-Schuman Limited 1982
This edition first published by Blackie 1986
Published in Puffin Books 1994
1 3 5 7 9 10 8 6 4 2

Filmset in Monophoto Garamond
Printed in England by Clays Ltd, St Ives plc

Contents

The File on Marmalade Atkins 9

Making plans for Marmalade 15

Marmalade at Eton 21

Marmalade in Venice 25

Marmalade's short stay at St Florinda's 33

Marmalade and Captain Crust 39

Marmalade mooches about 43

Marmalade and the Blessed Limit 49

Mrs Allgood has an idea 55

Marmalade blasts off 65

Marmalade and the Lord of the Universe 71

Marmalade and the Potman's Grotto 79

Some of you will have heard of Marmalade Atkins before, and some of you won't. If you have heard of Marmalade Atkins before, you will know that she was not a nice girl. In fact, many people thought that she was the worst girl in the world.

If you only like stories about nice little girls, do not read this book. You will be disgusted.

And if you like the sort of book in which bad girls learn to be good and happy, and a credit to their mummies and daddies, then this is not the sort of book for you either.

I am sorry about this, but there it is. Marmalade stays bad.

The File on Marmalade Atkins

If, like Marmalade Atkins, you are a very bad girl, you have an interesting time, and you meet some interesting people. Marmalade Atkins had wrecked the lives of a lot of interesting people, and they had got together the File on Marmalade Atkins.

A file is a sort of list of terrible things that a bad person has done, and a list of the things that people have thought up to try to make the bad person good.

By the time this story starts, the File on Marmalade Atkins was so big and fat that they had to carry it round in a wheelbarrow. If you want to read this story, it is only right that you should know some of the things they put in the File on Marmalade Atkins.

A lot of the Bad Things in the File on Marmalade Atkins have to do with a diabolical donkey called Rufus, who is not in this story. He was Marmalade Atkins's chief partner in crime, and here are some of the things they did together:

1   They tossed a posh snob called Cherith Ponsonby into a thistle patch and let the goat eat her new yellow riding boots.

2   They destroyed a valuable sofa and tried to pretend it was camels.

3   They completely demolished the El Poko Night Club and Restaurant.

4   They completely ruined the Nativity Play in Coventry Precinct, routed the Bulkington Silver Band, and were thoroughly beastly to a bunch of bishops.

If you really insist on knowing all the details of what Marmalade Atkins and Rufus did together, you will have to read a book called *Marmalade Atkins' Dreadful Deeds*.

But what about Rufus? you must be thinking. Especially those of you who know him. What's happened to him? Where's he gone? Why is he not going to be in this book?

Well, there are two stories about that. You will have to make up your minds which is the true one.

The first story is the one that Mr Atkins would tell you. Mr Atkins was Marmalade's father, and he was not a very nice man. He was not very fond of Marmalade and he was not very fond of Marmalade's mother, come to that. He was not very fond of anything, except leaning over fences in yellow and purple tweed suits poking pigs and saying

"Ar"; and he did like selling things. He sold things to rich people, and he was very good at it.

Selling things to rich people had practically made him into a millionaire. What did he sell to them? Anything he could think of: cars, pictures of sunsets, hamsters by the lorryload, and also, I am afraid, things that did not actually belong to him, such as Westminster Abbey and the Houses of Parliament. He did his level best to sell Marmalade Atkins as well, but no one was very enthusiastic.

After the bad business with the bishops, and the dreadful doings in the big city that followed, Mr Atkins decided that Rufus the donkey was not a good influence on his daughter, and that he would have to go. So he invited a bunch of rich people around, and to Marmalade's horror he auctioned Rufus to the highest bidder.

"The camel, we know, is the ship of the desert," he said, "but Rufus here will be the Rolls Royce of the Shifting Sands!"

The camel trader was very impressed indeed, and decided to pay Mr Atkins a large sum in gold. Rufus was packed into a strong wooden crate all ready to be flown off to the desert, and Mr Atkins staggered off to the bank with his pile of gold. That was the end of the story as far as he was concerned.

But late that night Marmalade Atkins was awakened by a sort of thumping sound, and then a sort of creaking sound, and then a sort of splintering sound. Almost, Marmalade thought, like the sounds you would hear if a small but powerful donkey was kicking his way out of a stout wooden crate.

And then there were some more sounds: some quiet clip-clopping, and a couple of moos, and then a lot of sharp tapping sounds, as if someone was nailing a stout wooden crate together again.

Then there was a gruff throaty sound halfway between a giant snoring and a gate creaking, and Marmalade opened her window to see her donkey standing in the middle of the yard.

"Rufus," she said. "You've escaped!"

"Course I 'ave, Marmalade Atkins. Don't fancy no desert, not me. And I done a deal with that young cow Elsie."

"What sort of deal?" said Marmalade.

"Well, she fancied seeing a bit of the world," said Rufus. "Cows don't see much of the world. Dull life, cows 'ave. This way, see, she gets a trip in an executive jet plane, get a look at a bit of desert like. Camel trader gets narked he's got a cow not a donkey, and he'll send 'er back 'ome. Laugh'll be on your dad then, eh?" And Rufus let out a hoarse metallic guffaw.

"But what are you going to do?" said Marmalade.

"Ah well," said Rufus. "Have to make meself scarce for a bit. Going on a trip, like."

"Where?"

"Not sayin'."

"Take me with you!"

"Not this trip, Marmalade Atkins," said Rufus. "I need you to stay here, keep things going like. Put yourself about a bit on your own. If you need any help, there's always the nodding bloodhound."

"Always the what?"

"Cheerio, Marmalade Atkins!"

And Rufus trotted out of the yard away into the darkness and out of this book.

Making plans for Marmalade

After Mr Atkins had got rid of Rufus the donkey by selling him to the camel trader, he was extremely pleased with himself. He was often to be seen wandering round the grounds singing snatches of old folk-songs in a very loud and tuneless voice, which irritated his wife so much that she ordered four new fur coats from Harrods to spite him.

Mr Atkins did not seem to notice this at all, however. He was spending more and more time leaning over the wall in his tweed hat and leggings, poking his pig Rover, and saying things like, "Ar. This be the loife," and "Nice bit of bacon, that," over and over again. This got on Rover's nerves more than somewhat. He hated being poked, and what was more, he thought that talking about bacon was very tactless.

Marmalade Atkins sympathised with Rover's point of view, and one day she unlatched Rover's gate.

When Mr Atkins came home that evening after a hard day at work, he leaned over the gate and gave Rover an especially hard poke in the bottom, saying: "Ar, me old beauty. Lovely bit of cracklin' there!" Rover the Free Range Pig, who had had a bit of a hard day himself, poked back, and found to his delight that the gate swung open.

"Whoa there, me old darlin'!" said Mr Atkins in a very nervous way, but Rover was in a mood for poking, not whoaing, and he chased Mr Atkins all the way to the house and up the stairs, where Mr Atkins locked himself in the bathroom.

Mr Atkins had a very boring evening in the bathroom, because Mrs Atkins thought it was his own fault and pretended not to hear his cries for help. Eventually Marmalade Atkins persuaded her father to escape through the bathroom window, which he did with some difficulty, tearing all the buttons off his expensive tweed suit, and then falling into a pile of manure which he had been meaning to put on the rose garden.

Rover the Free Range Pig trotted downstairs and strolled round to watch with Marmalade as Mr Atkins slowly emerged from the manure heap, shaking tufty brown lumps from his pockets, eyebrows and ears.

"This be the loife, eh, mate?" said Marmalade Atkins to Rover the Free Range Pig, which made Mr Atkins wonder if his daughter might have had something to do with the incident.

He made his smelly way back to the bathroom, had a

bath, then a shower, then another bath, and then splashed himself all over with Marmalade's mother's very best perfume, which had cost fifty pounds a bottle. Mr Atkins used three bottles of it, which made him feel a lot better. Then he put on his purple silk smoking jacket. He had decided to go to the smoking room, smoke a cigar, and have a serious think about Marmalade Atkins and what to do about her.

But when he opened the cigar cupboard, there were no cigars! Empty box after empty box, which had once held priceless Havana cigars.

"Darling! Sweetypie!" he called in a voice of savage fury.

"Yes, my poppet?" hissed Mrs Atkins from the kitchen.

"Have you been smoking my cigars at all?"

"Not at all. Not one little bit! In point of fact I loathe and detest them!" said Mrs Atkins. "And you," she added in a voice only slightly less loud.

"Just asking, sweetypie," said Mr Atkins.

"Marmalade!"

"Yes, cock?" said Marmalade, coming into the smoking room.

"Do you know anything about my cigars?"

"Father," said Marmalade. "I cannot tell a lie. I gave them to the goat and he ate them."

Mr Atkins slowly took off his smoking jacket, tore it into two pieces, threw the pieces on the floor and stamped on them.

After doing this, he was able to control himself enough to ask, in a voice trembling with rage, "Marmalade, why did you let the goat eat my Havana cigars?"

"Well," said Marmalade, "I couldn't get him to smoke them."

Mr Atkins stared at her for a few seconds and then began to jump up and down, making curious strangled sounds in his throat, and Marmalade decided that it would probably be a good idea to go for a walk.

When Mr Atkins had recovered a little he went into the kitchen, where Mrs Atkins sat eating a couple of boxes of liqueur chocolates. She looked hot and irritable and rather fat. This was because she was wearing all her fur coats at once in an effort to annoy her husband. But to her disappointment he still didn't notice. He only thought about one thing at a time, and he was thinking about Marmalade.

"Think we ought to do something about that girl," he said. "She's getting up my nose."

"What a curious pastime for a young girl," said Mrs Atkins. "And doomed to failure. Your nose is very big my dear, but hardly that big!" Mrs Atkins laughed loudly and recklessly at her witty sally. I am sorry to say that she had eaten so many liqueur chocolates that she was not quite sober.

"I wonder if I could sell her to one of my clients," said Mr Atkins.

"Atkins," said his wife. "You are a fine salesman, but

you could not sell a girl like Marmalade to a rag-and-bone merchant. Besides, I understand it's against the law to sell little girls."

"Pettifogging rules and regulations," said Mr Atkins. "No wonder this country's going down the plughole. Well, what's to be done with her?"

"A new school," said Mrs Atkins. "A Top Security School, a long way away. Somewhere oldfashioned, where they still cane them, and roast them over open fires. I really do feel that's what our daughter needs, Atkins."

"Good thinking, sweetypie," said Mr Atkins, brightening. "And if I slip them a few quid extra, maybe they'll keep her for the holidays, too."

Marmalade at Eton

Mr Atkins asked his rich clients if they knew of any good schools. They all said the same thing.

"Eton, old boy," they said. "Went there meself. Fine place. Very strict, very smart: stiff collars, striped trousers, bum-freezers. Just the job, old boy."

Mr Atkins liked the sound of Eton, especially the bum-freezers. He didn't know what they were but he was sure they would do Marmalade a world of good.

So one fine afternoon he dressed up in a black coat, striped trousers and top hat, and set off with Marmalade in the Rolls Royce. On the way he kept sneaking glances at his daughter, who was wearing muddy jeans and a teeshirt with a picture of a donkey on it. Somehow, he thought, this would not go down well at Eton College, so he made a detour and stopped off at Moss Bros, a posh shop in London where they can make you look smart no matter what size and shape you happen to be.

"Black coat, striped trousers, stiff collar for the girl here," he said. The men in Moss Bros giggled a lot at first, but when Mr Atkins pulled out a handful of fifty-pound notes they soon bustled about, and there was Marmalade looking like a small and evil-tempered waiter.

"And a top hat," said Mr Atkins as an afterthought.

The top hat came down over Marmalade's ears and hid most of her face, which was not a bad thing on the whole, or so Mr Atkins thought.

The headmaster of Eton was rather alarmed when Mr Atkins and Marmalade came marching into his study. But he had seen a lot of strange things in his time, and was well known for his good manners, so he simply asked Mr Atkins what he wanted.

"Hear you run a fine school here, old boy," said Mr Atkins. "Bum-freezers, stiff collars, all that, Mrs Atkins and I have decided to let you have a go at Marmalade."

"You are too kind," said the headmaster, "but I have all the marmalade I need at present."

"Listen, cock," said Marmalade. "I'm Marmalade, and no funny cracks if you don't mind."

"Ah," said the headmaster. "What an unusual and charming name. But I am sorry to say that we have no vacancies at present. In fact, Mr Atkins, we have a twenty year waiting list."

"We can't wait that long!" said Mr Atkins. "Look, I don't mind paying a bit over the odds. And there's a few tenners in it for you personally, know what I mean?"

"Are you trying to bribe me, Mr Atkins?"

"Of course I am, we're desperate to get rid of her!"

The headmaster froze.

"*Her?* Is that a *girl?*"

"Run the clippers over her head," said Mr Atkins. "No one'll be any the wiser."

"My dear Mr Atkins," said the headmaster. "There are no vacancies; if there were any vacancies they would not be for girls; and if we took girls I doubt very much if your daughter would be clev.. enough for Eton College."

"Oh yeah?" said Marmalade. She didn't want to go to Eton, but she was getting fed up with all this. "You tell me this, cock. What is the difference between a Dobermann Pinscher and a Piecost?"

The headmaster of Eton is, of course, one of the cleverest men in England, but somehow he couldn't seem to think of an answer. He scratched his head hopefully for a moment or two, and then said:

"Er . . . what's a Piecost, Marmalade?"

"About ninety pee in the chipshop," said Marmalade. "Gotcha! Come, fathah! This man is not clevah enough to educate your daughtah!"

And out she went.

"Shame we couldn't do business," said Mr Atkins. "Would have been a few bob in it for you, I know you teachers don't get much pay."

And he followed his daughter out to the Rolls.

The headmaster sat down trembling for a few minutes.

He thought about setting the Eton College Beagle Pack on to Mr Atkins and Marmalade, but after a moment or two he realised that if he just sat there like a good quiet headmaster he would never have to see Mr Atkins or Marmalade again. So that was what he did.

"This is a sorry tale," said Marmalade's mother when they got home. "I should never have left things to you, Atkins. Now, I have heard of an excellent finishing school for young ladies. One of the excellent things about it is that it is a long way from here."

"How far?" said Marmalade.

"Well, quite far," said her mother. "Italy, actually. Place called Venice. Ever so pretty. Lots of canals, gondolas, ice cream . . . you'll love it, darling."

Marmalade in Venice

Marmalade did not love it at the Bandolini Finishing School for Young Ladies, and the Bandolini School for Young Ladies did not love Marmalade.

The lady in charge of the Bandolini Finishing School was a very short fat lady called Signora Bandolini, who always wore very tight shiny dresses made of black silk. Marmalade Atkins thought she looked remarkably like a fat black beetle in high heels.

"You look just like a fat black beetle in high heels," said Marmalade to Signora Bandolini on her first morning. It was then that Signora Bandolini began to think that she might have bitten off more than she could chew.

"This girl gotta lotsa problems," she said to herself.

"Well, cock," said Marmalade. "At least I haven't got your problem. Your problem is, you look like a beetle."

The Bandolini Finishing school was not like ordinary schools. It did have all the ordinary things schools have, such as sums and writing and maps and school dinners, but it also had special things to turn the girls into ladies. These special things were called Manners, Deportment, and Culture.

Manners was learning to eat spaghetti without slurping. When the Bandolini girls ate their spaghetti, it was a wondrous sight: forty dainty daughters of the rich, all curling spaghetti round their forks, and slipping the long snaky strands into their prim little mouths without a single sound, while Signora Bandolini walked up and down the rows between the tables in carpet slippers, dropping pins on to the polished floor, making sure she heard every single one.

That was what it was like before Marmalade Atkins's arrival. Marmalade was fond of spaghetti, but she had her own ways of dealing with it.

"Through the teeth and round the gums,
    Look out stomach, here it comes!"
cried Marmalade, and set to work as though she were in a wrestling match with a mad octopus. Spaghetti whirled around her head like dancing worms, and the air was full of a damp mist of brown juice.

"That's the way to do it!" yelled Marmalade as a particularly long strand of spaghetti flew off like a whiplash and hung from the chandelier. "Have a go, girls!"

The dainty daughters of the rich looked at her in horror,

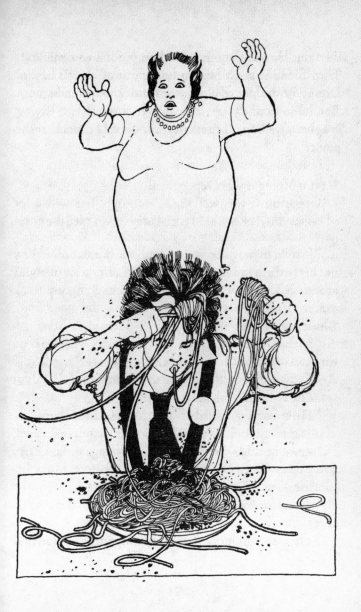

then one by one they timidly tried out the new method. They found it great fun. In no time at all the Bandolini Dining Room looked like a rope factory, and poor Signora Bandolini dashed up and down through the flying spaghetti wailing, "I canta hear the pinsa! I canta hear the pinsa!"

Next morning it was Deportment.

Deportment was walking in a straight line with a lot of books on your head. Marmalade couldn't see the point of it.

"Listen, mate," she said to Signora Bandolini. "Why not carry them in a bag, if you have to carry a lot of books around? Take my advice, people are going to think you're barmy, going round with books on your head. Blimey, they'll say—"

"Silence," screamed Signora Bandolini. "The books on the head teach you to walka like a lady. It is very hard to do. And I, Signora Bandolini, I am the champion of all Italy at walking with the books on the head!"

"How many can you do?" said Marmalade Atkins.

A faraway look came into Signora Bandolini's eyes. "Once," she said, "when I am still a younga girla, I carry forty-three bigga booksa on the head, before Mussolini himselfa."

"Good for you, Beetle," said Marmalade. "Bet I can do forty-four."

"Ha!" said Signora Bandolini, forgetting her ladylike

manners. "I like-a see you try, little scratty English baddy!"

They needed a very tall stepladder to load the forty-four big books on Marmalade's head. Long before the last one was in place, Marmalade was beginning to feel like a tent peg being hammered into the ground. Perhaps this was why Signora Bandolini was so short and fat : squashed by the bigga booksa.

At last all the books were in place. Signora Bandolini looked a very long way away at the far end of the hall, and even more like a black beetle.

"OK!" shouted Signora Bandolini. "Deportamenta begin!"

Marmalade did really rather well for the first few steps, and then the huge pile of books began to shift forwards. Marmalade quickened her pace, but so did the books. They seemed determined to reach the end of the hall before Marmalade Atkins did. Marmalade broke into a run.

A look of terror came over Signora Bandolini's face as she realised what was going to happen, but it was too late.

Marmalade skidded to a halt three feet in front of Signora Bandolini, the forty-four books curled over in a graceful arc like a waterfall, and Signora Bandolini disappeared beneath them with a despairing howl.

"Sorry, cock," said Marmalade Atkins. "You win."

The Deportment lesson was over.

Next day it was Culture.

Culture was trooping round museums going "ooh" and "ah" at paintings, and it was also boat trips round the islands of the Venice lagoon going "ooh" and "ah" at the wonders of nature.

The girls had a guide, whose name was Signora Nora, the Eurohols Fun Girl. She thought everything was super, and very lovely and typical, and very turistico and characteristico.

They watched a glass blower blow glass ("very very lovely and typical, very very turistico," said Signora Nora) and saw a gondolier fall out of his gondola ("not to be missedico," said Marmalade Atkins).

After a while Marmalade became very very bored with Signora Nora. After failing to disconnect Signora Nora's loudspeaker, she noticed an interesting looking knob on the bottom of the boat.

"Just give it a twistico," said Marmalade. "And a flick of the wristico. . ."

The knob flew out of the bottom of the boat and a great deal of water came in. Signora Nora was so carried away with how lovely and typical everything was that she didn't realise what was happening until the water was over her loudspeaker and the girls were diving over the side like deserting rats.

Fortunately no lives were lost.

Marmalade Atkins was sent home next day with her school report. It was quite short, and went like this:

Bandolini Finishing School for Young Ladies
Principale : Signora Bandolini
Report on Marmalade Atkins
Manners   0
Deportment   0
Culture   0
We have finish with this girl.

Eleonora Bandolini

Marmalade's short stay at St Florinda's

Marmalade's mother and father were surprised and disappointed to see Marmalade back so soon. In fact, as soon as Mr Atkins read Signora Bandolini's report, he said, "Sensible woman, that Bandolini. *We have finish with her*, eh? Got a fine ring about it, that has. Well I have finish with her too. Either she goes, or I do."

"Cheerio, cock," said Marmalade. "Don't forget to send us a postcard!"

Mr Atkins suddenly realised that it was in fact a lot easier for him to go than to find another boarding school for Marmalade, so he jumped into his Rolls Royce and tootled off to London. I would like to be able to say that he worried about leaving Marmalade and Mrs Atkins to cope with things on their own, but I cannot tell a lie. In fact he forgot about Marmalade and Mrs Atkins before his car was even out of the gate.

Mrs Atkins was not at all pleased. She was quite glad that Mr Atkins had gone off, because she thought he was rather a waste of space at the best of times, but she was not at all thrilled at the prospect of her daughter's company. None of her friends would come round to play bridge if they knew Marmalade was going to be there. Even the postman and the milkman tended to stay away.

She picked up the telephone and dialled the number of St Florinda's. St Florinda's was a fine old British Boarding School for Girls with no nonsense about it. No Deportment, no Culture, not much to eat, come to that, but lots and lots of lacrosse.

Lacrosse, in case you have not come across it in your own school, is a rather daft game not unlike hockey, except that you play it with a string bag on the end of your stick. Well, they were very keen on lacrosse at St Florinda's, which was usually known as St Floss for short. The headmistress of St Floss, whose name was Miss Bloss, thought that there was nothing like lacrosse for building the characters of British girls and making them sturdy and fearless and a credit to the school. She had a school motto that went like this :
"A girl is never at a loss
when she has learnt to play lacrosse."

Miss Bloss was delighted to hear that Mrs Atkins wanted to send Marmalade to St Floss, even though Mrs Atkins did her best to warn her.

"She's rather a problem, I'm afraid," said Marmalade's mother. "People don't take to her."

"Shy, is she?" said Miss Bloss. "Lacrosse will take care of that."

"Well," said Mrs Atkins. "It's more that she makes other people shy."

"Oh, don't you worry, Mrs Atkins," boomed Miss Bloss down the telephone wires. "You know what we say at St Floss:
Plenty of lackers will do the trick;
A girl's best friend is her lackers stick!
    Put her on the next train!"

Marmalade arrived at St Florinda's next day, and was sent straight to the lacrosse field, where Miss Bloss was booming away at a lot of little girls with lacrosse sticks.

Miss Bloss was a tall plump jolly old girl with very interesting hair. It was piled high on her head, and looked, Marmalade thought, like a cross between a cottage loaf and a bird's nest.

"Welcome to St Florinda's, Marmalade dear," said Miss Bloss. "I'm sure you'll be happy here, but if anything bothers you, just ask me!"

"There is one thing bothering me," said Marmalade. "What's that on your head, a cottage loaf or a bird's nest?"

Miss Bloss felt just a little bit uneasy for a moment. But then she recovered. Lacrosse would do the trick, of course it would!

"Don't be personal, dear. Just get stuck into the lackers, you'll soon pick it up."

Marmalade soon picked it up, but she could not see what all the fuss was about. She tried using her stick as a butterfly net, then held it up to her face and growled at Miss Bloss through the netting like a caged leopard, but Miss Bloss wisely ignored this.

Bored, Marmalade wandered off to the side of the pitch, where the school cat, a stout and adventurous young grey job called Foggy, trotted up to her and jumped into the string bag of Marmalade's lacrosse stick, rolling about in it like a drunken sailor in a hammock. This gave Marmalade an idea.

"Have you ever wished you could fly through the air, Foggy?" she said.

"Prrow?" said Foggy, who was game for most things.

Marmalade took a quick sighting on Miss Bloss, who was blowing on a fat silver whistle at the far end of the field. Then she whirled the net round her head three times, and launched Foggy on her maiden flight. The school cat skimmed gracefully over the heads of the astonished lacrosse players like a fat grey rocket, and homed in on Miss Bloss's hairdo as if magnetised.

"Goal!" yelled Marmalade.

"Help," yelled Miss Bloss, stumbling about in a panic with the cat's paws over her eyes.

"Prrow!" said Foggy, who had greatly enjoyed both the flight and the landing, and leapt off Miss Bloss's head into the hammock stick of a short fierce girl called Amabel Pratt, clearly ready for another daredevil flight.

"Shoot!" said Marmalade. Amabel Pratt shot, and Foggy landed for the second time on Miss Bloss's cottage-loaf-bird's-nest.

"Prrow!" said Foggy. A new sport had been born.

In the end Marmalade's team won by seven goals to five, Foggy became the hero of all the local cats, and Miss Bloss decided to retire from her job and live with her sister in Menorca, where they have never heard of lacrosse. As she tottered into the taxi, people near enough to hear said she was muttering:

"I was totally wrong about lackers,
And now it has driven me crackers."

I ought to add a word about Foggy the school cat. After the lacrosse episode Foggy went on to become a famous stunt cat, sitting on motorcyclists' heads as they jumped over buses, diving off towers into bowls of milk, and so on.

What I am getting at is that Foggy was not your usual sort of cat. If you were daft enough to try playing lacrosse with your school cat, she would whack you across the chops if not worse. You have been warned.

Marmalade and Captain Crust

Even Marmalade's father had his doubts about sending his little girl to Captain Crust's Mountain Training School for Boys and Girls. Captain Crust's Mountain Training School was said by many to be the toughest school in Britain. "Make 'em or break 'em," was Captain Crust's motto, and he would sometimes add: "an I dinna care verra much which I do!"

"Look here, mate," said Marmalade to her father, as they studied the prospectus that had come in the post that morning, "I don't like the look of this place at all."

On the front page of the prospectus was a picture of a very fierce-looking man in a vest and a kilt, surrounded by guard dogs. On his vest was written *Make 'em or break 'em!* and in the background you could see a lot of starved but tough-looking boys and girls carrying treetrunks up mountains.

Inside it told you all the things you could do at Captain Crust's: scale cliffs, swim in icy rivers, stalk wildcats, and so on. There wasn't anything about sums, or deportment, or lacrosse, but what there was sounded terrible.

"Look," said Marmalade. "You can't send me there. I mean, what if it breaks me? I mean, how would *you* like it?"

"I wouldn't like it a bit," admitted Mr Atkins ruefully. Then he brightened up. "Still," he said, "I'm not the one who's going, am I?"

Captain Crust's Mountain Training School was so far up into the mountains that it took fourteen hours in a Land-drover to get there. The school consisted of a few wooden shacks for the children and the guard dogs, and a huge luxury caravan, where Captain Crust himself lived with cupboards full of haggis and de luxe whisky.

Captain Crust had the reddest and hairiest knees that Marmalade had ever seen, as he stepped down from his luxury caravan to welcome her.

"Now, me bonnie wee lassie," he said. "I am Captain Crust, ye ken, and I'm tough as old boots. And you ken what I'm going to do with ye? I'm going to gralloch ye and whip-ma-whap-ma ye till you're as tough as old boots as well. Any questions?"

"Yes," said Marmalade. "Why are your knees so red and hairy?"

"Because I am such a terrible terrible man!" roared Captain Crust, and even Marmalade felt alarmed. "Now

away to your bread and water and your hard wooden bed," he went on, "for at dawn we begin on the making and the breaking!"

And at dawn they began. On her first day at Captain Crust's Mountain Training School Marmalade Atkins climbed two mountains, felled three mighty trees, swam four icy rivers, ate five bowls of watery porridge, and made friends with one of the guard dogs.

On her second day she clambered down two slimy potholes, staggered through three bogs, came fourteenth in the school caber-tossing competition, led a protest about the school meals and got gralloched by Captain Crust . . . and made friends with two more of the guard dogs.

On the third day Marmalade Atkins led the Great Escape. The full details of the escape are a secret to this day, but I can tell you that they had a lot to do with treacle, haggis, and half-sawn tree trunks.

In all, forty-three boys and girls escaped from Captain Crust's Mountain Training School. Fifteen of the boys and girls and two of the dogs were never recaptured. They are said to be still living wild in caves, and if you are ever on holiday in a part of Scotland known as the Trossachs you might like to keep an eye open for them. (You will know them by their red hairy knees).

Marmalade mooches about

After her Great Escape from Captain Crust's Mountain Training School, Marmalade spent most of her time mooching about at home, which suited her fine.

She mooched down to the pig-pen and let out Rover the Free Range Pig, and took him for a walk. They mooched down to the paddock to see Torchy and Gypsy, the two horses. Torchy, the fat white pony, was rolling on his back kicking his legs in the air and enjoying the sun on his fat white belly. He often did this, and sometimes when people were trying to ride on his back. Marmalade didn't blame him. That was what she would probably do if people were trying to ride on her back.

"You carry on, mate," she said to Torchy. "It's a free country."

It wasn't a free country, though. That was the trouble. If you were a horse people kept getting on your back and whacking you, if you were a pig people kept putting you in a pig-pen and poking you, and if you were a girl they kept sending you to schools and mucking about with your brain.

Take Gypsy. Gypsy was a lovely character to talk to, mild, friendly, fond of a stroke and a nuzzle. It was only when you got on his back that he became Mad Gypsy Atkins, got the Red Mist, and ran at full speed into any obstacle that was in his way. He trotted up now, had an affable sniffing conversation with Rover, then let Marmalade tickle his lower lip until all his teeth showed in a huge horsy grin.

"All right, mate," said Marmalade. "Nobody's going to get on your back today."

The two horses and Rover mooched off to the orchard to eat windfalls, and Marmalade mooched off to the back yard. The back yard was a mess. It was full of the remains of Mr Atkins's bright ideas: a broken down tractor from the days when he thought he would like to be a real farmer, a broken down rowing machine from the days when he thought he would really Get Fit, and a broken down Dormobile from the days when he used to take his family on holidays.

Marmalade climbed into the old Dormobile and bounced around for a bit on the squeaky old seats. She liked the old Dormobile. You could have a mooch and a think and imagine you were zooming down the motorways a million miles away from Mr and Mrs Atkins. You didn't have to be bad in there and you didn't have to be good. You could just be ordinary, and no one would muck you about.

Marmalade lolled on the back seat, poking with her toe at the nodding bloodhound who sat peacefully in the back window. You used to see a lot of nodding dogs, Alsatians mostly, in the back windows of people's cars. When the car is moving, the nodding dog's head goes wiggling up and down. If you have to drive for a long time behind a car with a nodding dog in the back, the nodding drives you barmy after a while. This, of course, was why Mr Atkins had bought the nodding bloodhound. He liked to drive people barmy.

But this Dormobile had not moved for years, and now the nodding bloodhound only nodded if you gave him a prod. It was strangely soothing to lie there on the back seat, thinking about nothing and watching his gloomy old chops go up and down, up and down. . .

"That's it, Marmalade Atkins. Keep your pecker up."

What was that? Had the nodding bloodhound spoken to her? Impossible. He was a toy. You could even see how he was made, just a lot of plastic and metal and fake fur. Up and down, up and down . . . She must have nodded off herself.

Then she remembered something Rufus had said before he went off on his travels. "If you need any help, there's always the nodding bloodhound."

Ridiculous. What sort of help could you expect from something that wasn't even alive?

"What sort of help are you going to be then?" said Marmalade to the nodding bloodhound, feeling rather silly.

Of course there was no reply. Up and down went his gloomy old chops, up and down, up and down.

All the same, thought Marmalade, you had to pay attention to what Rufus the Donkey said, so she took the nodding bloodhound back to the house, and gave him a new home on her bedroom windowsill next to her Dracula model.

"There you are, me old mate," she said. "Nod away. It's a free country."

When she came downstairs, she had a nasty shock. Sitting on the living room sofa was Mrs Nora Allgood. Mrs Allgood was, as she always said, in one of the Helping Professions, and was famous for her Understanding Smiles, and the Way she had with Problem Children. Marmalade couldn't stand her.

"Hello, Marmalade dear," said Mrs Allgood, trying out one of her special smiles. "I hear we've been rather naughty again."

"Oh, we have, have we?" said Marmalade. "What naughty things have you been up to then?"

"Don't be vile, Marmalade," said her mother automatically.

"When I say 'we' dear, I mean *you*," said Mrs Allgood. Her Understanding Smile had begun to droop on one side. "Still," she went on brightly, "let's put all that behind us. I've got some rather wonderful news!"

"I know," said Marmalade. "My dad's sold you to one of his clients.

"No dear," said Mrs Allgood. "Sister Conception and Sister Purification have been in touch with me."

(Sister Conception and Sister Purification were in charge of the Convent of the Sacred Heart, one of the many schools Marmalade had been asked to leave. If you have read a book called *Marmalade Atkins' Dreadful Deeds* you will know about the dreadful things Marmalade did there.)

"Sister Conception and Sister Purification," Mrs Allgood went on, "have done something very very lovely."

"I know," said Marmalade. "They've burnt the school down."

"No dear," said Mrs Allgood. "They have forgiven you. They're going to take you back, Marmalade!"

Marmalade and the Blessed Limit

Sister Conception and Sister Purification were a couple of very tough nuns, and they ran a very tight convent. You may have known some nuns, and some of them might have been tough, but Sister Conception and Sister Purification were special.

For a start, they were both over six feet tall. Sister Purification could give you a look that would reduce most bad girls to quivering jellies, and Sister Conception had a moustache and did weight training. They had tamed so many bad girls that their school was known as the Convent of the Blessed Limit. They would never admit that they were beaten. Being nuns, they were also very hot on forgiving people, letting bygones be bygones, and giving even very bad girls One Last Chance. But by the end of a week, they had had enough of Marmalade Atkins.

By the end of a week, Marmalade Atkins had done the following things:

She had sewed Sister Conception to the altar cloth in needlework.

She had crept up behind three very good girls called Eileen Rogan, Eileen Hogan, and Eileen Gogan, and tied them together by their pigtails so tightly that they had had to go round for days like Siamese triplets.

She had swopped round the music for the choir so that instead of singing the 23rd Psalm they sang, "I've got a lovely bunch of coconuts!"

She had put a small crocodile in the swimming pool. The crocodile had not actually eaten anybody, but it had been a very narrow escape for Mary McSharry, who has nightmares about it to this day.

After the crocodile episode, the Head Girl, a posh snob called Cherith Ponsonby, was ordered to go with Marmalade everywhere she went, to make sure that she did not do any more Bad Things. Cherith Ponsonby had always got on Marmalade's nerves, and it was too much to expect Marmalade to put up with her company all day. Or so Marmalade thought. I am sorry to say that at the end of the day poor Cherith Ponsonby was found to be Superglued to the toilet seat.

Sister Conception and Sister Purification called Marmalade to the office to give her a Serious Talking-to.

Now most girls would be terrified out of their wits if Sister Conception and Sister Purification gave them a Talking-to. Sister Purification had eyes that could bore into you like laser beams, and Sister Conception when she was cross had a roar like a maddened bull. Just the sight of the two enormous nuns, sitting on their high stools so that they looked even more enormous, would be enough to make most people want to curl up and die of shame and fright.

"Marmalade Atkins!" said Sister Purification.

"Yes, cock?" said Marmalade.

"Yes, sister!" thundered Sister Conception.

"Suit yourself, cock," said Marmalade.

Sister Conception, flying into one of her instant rages, picked up a baseball bat in her hairy fist.

"Be patient, Sister Conception," said Sister Purification. "She is only a little child."

"Ooh, I'd love to give her one!" rumbled Sister Conception. "Knock that cheeky grin right off her—"

"Sister, sister!"

Sister Conception subsided, muttering and growling to herself.

"Marmalade Atkins," said Sister Purification, and her voice was sharp and cold as an ice-axe. "How many schools have you been asked to leave?"

"You tell me," said Marmalade Atkins.

"I *will* tell you. *Ten!*"

"Is it a record?" said Marmalade.

"Be silent, girl!" said Sister Conception, brandishing the baseball bat.

"Sorry, cock."

"And don't call me cock!"

"Now, Marmalade," said Sister Purification. "What

they say about us is that we never give up. We are never beaten. But after this terrible week, I have my doubts."

"Give her to me!" roared Sister Conception. "I'll give her some hammer!"

"Before we decide on your punishment," said Sister Purification, "have you got anything to say? Are you not ashamed of yourself, Marmalade Atkins?"

There was a short silence. Marmalade was thinking. The two nuns allowed themselves to hope. Perhaps, at last, she *was* ashamed of herself. Perhaps she was even going to say she was sorry!

"Listen, mate," said Marmalade Atkins at last. "The way I see it, it's very simple. No hard feelings. But it's my *job* to muck about, and it's your job to try and stop me. I mean, that's what school *is*, isn't it?"

Sister Purification and Sister Conception stared at each other. Neither of them had thought of this idea before, and somehow neither of them could think of the answer to it. They sat there on their high stools opening and shutting their mouths, but no words came out.

"What's the matter? Lost your tongues?"

"Come away, sister," said Sister Purification, and the the two baffled nuns swept out of the office. It was then that they discovered that their stools had been Super-glued to their bottoms.

Mrs Allgood has an idea

In the middle of the night Marmalade sat up suddenly. She didn't know why she had woken up. She was not even quite sure that she *was* awake. In the faint light she could see the silhouette of the nodding bloodhound nodding quietly away to himself on the window sill. Very peaceful, very reassuring, to think of him nodding the night away. Wait a minute. How could he be nodding *by himself*? Rufus had been right, she thought. There was more to this bloodhound than met the eye.

Downstairs she could hear voices. Her mother. Her father. And someone else.

It didn't sound like one of her father's rich clients. It didn't sound like one of her mother's awful friends. It sounded worse. It sounded like Mrs Allgood.

"I'm going down there," said Marmalade. "Better see what they're up to. Might be a plot."

"You do that thing, Marmalade Atkins," said the nodding bloodhound.

Marmalade turned and stared. Had he said that or was she dreaming? "Come again, cock," she said.

But the nodding bloodhound just lay there nodding his gloomy old chops. She must have imagined it.

Marmalade crept out of bed and put her slippers on. As usual when she woke up in the night, she felt a bit peckish, so she tiptoed down the stairs and went into the pantry. She found six cold sausages, ate four of them, put two in her pyjama pocket for emergencies, then tiptoed to the doorway of the living room.

Strange. It was the middle of the night upstairs but in the living room it seemed to be daytime. There was her father in a bright green tracksuit panting after an exhausting jog round the house. There was her mother in one of her dreadful posh dresses, stabbing away savagely at a bit of embroidery.

And there on the sofa, wearing her best Understanding Smile (she did have her clothes on as well) sat the dreaded Mrs Allgood, chomping away at a plate of Marmalade's favourite chocolate biscuits.

Marmalade had the urge to rush roaring into the living room, snatch the biscuits, and make a dash for freedom with them, but for once she controlled herself. She wanted to hear what they were talking about. She wriggled herself behind the grandfather clock and listened. And this is what she heard.

"So," said Mr Atkins. "Our little girl has been getting up the nuns' noses, is that the form?"

"Well, not literally, Mr Atkins," said Mrs Allgood, through a mouthful of chocolate biscuit. "She *has* been extremely difficult."

"Not surprised," said Mr Atkins. "She gets up her mother's nose. Gets up *my* nose. Gets up everyone's nose."

"I *wish* you wouldn't use that expression, darling," said Mrs Atkins.

I get up the *wife's* nose, y'see," said Mr Atkins. "*She* gets up *my* nose, come to that. We're what you might call a problem family. Good job I'm not home very often, eh?"

"Hear, hear!" agreed Mrs Atkins with a shrill hysterical laugh. "Don't you think he's the absolute end, Mrs Allgood?"

"Well, I hardly know what to say," said Mrs Allgood. (In fact she privately thought that the whole Atkins family were the absolute end, but she was too polite to say so; and she did enjoy their chocolate biscuits.)

"Of course," went on Mrs Atkins, "he is practically a millionaire, and one can overlook a lot for that. But he really is an absolute pig. I mean, what sort of man would name his own daughter Marmalade?"

"Nothing wrong with Marmalade, perfectly ordinary name," said Mr Atkins. Then he sprang up and unzipped his bright green tracksuit. Mrs Allgood, who was rather prim, shut her eyes for a moment, but when she opened them again she saw that underneath he was wearing his business suit.

"Well," said Mr Atkins. "Nothing I'd like better than to sit round chewing the fat with you ladies, but I must be off to work."

"Don't let us keep you, darling," said Mrs Atkins affectionately. "I'm sure Mrs Allgood is as sick of the sight of you as I am."

"Jolly good," said Marmalade's father.

"No, no!" cried Mrs Allgood. "Don't go yet, please, Mr Atkins. I shall need your consent!"

"What for?" said Mr Atkins suspiciously. Behind the grandfather clock, Marmalade pricked up her ears. This must be important.

"Well," said Mrs Allgood, licking chocolate off the end of her nose, "your daughter, as you know, has *very serious problems.*"

"She doesn't *have* problems," said Mrs Atkins. "She *is* a problem. No one knows what to do with her."

"You can say that again," said Mr Atkins.

"Mr Atkins bought me a lovely pair of earplugs," said Marmalade's mother, "but I could still *see* her. And then we went off on a world cruise and left her behind. That was quite successful, but when we came back, there she was again. *And* she'd invited a lot of donkeys and goats to stay, and they'd absolutely wrecked the furniture, as well as eating most of my hats."

Mrs Atkins nodded glumly. "Tried the crocodile then. Fat lot of good *he* was."

"Crocodile?" gasped Mrs Allgood. She had not heard about the crocodile.

"Yes, just a small one," said Mrs Atkins. "He came all the way from Africa in a little wooden box. I bought him a collar and called him Prince. I thought he'd keep her in order. Not a bit of good. They got on like a house on fire! She took him to school and set him on the nuns!"

Mrs Allgood took a deep breath.

"Mr and Mrs Atkins," she said. "I think I may have the solution to your problems. You may perhaps have heard of Intermediate Treatment—IT, as we call it in the Helping Professions?"

"Sounds a bit mild for Marmalade," said Mr Atkins doubtfully.

"Exactly," said Mrs Allgood, taking another biscuit. "That's why what I'm recommending for Marmalade is not IT but *VET*!"

"VET?"

"Very Extreme Treatment," said Mrs Allgood. "It's quite new. It's a little bit like Outward Bound . . . only more so."

"I see, jolly good," said Mr Atkins. "So what do you do with the little beggars?"

"Blast them off into space," said Mrs Allgood. "Those who return are completely changed for the better."

"Those who return?" said Mr Atkins keenly.

"Yes," said Mrs Allgood. "I think it's only fair to point out that you may never see your daughter Marmalade again."

There was a short pause.

"Can we have that in writing?" said Mr Atkins.

Marmalade decided that it was time to make an appearance.

"Just a minute, cock!" she said, leaping out from behind the clock brandishing a sausage. "I heard all that!"

"Oh, hello, Marmalade dear," said Mrs Allgood nervously. "Doesn't she look sweet in her pyjamas?"

"Huh!" said Mrs Atkins bitterly.

"We were just discussing your problems, dear," said Mrs Allgood.

Marmalade sat down next to her, moved the biscuits out of her reach, and took one herself.

"I'm not deaf, cock!" she said. "You were just discussing blasting me off into space!"

"Sounds like the chance of a lifetime," said her father cheerily.

"What exactly happens?" said Marmalade suspiciously.

"Well, as I say," said Mrs Allgood, "it's all a bit experimental, so no one's quite sure. The idea is to make you into a *good girl,* and you sometimes hear the process called *brainwashing.* Washing out the bad, and washing in the good. It'll be a bit like an adventure, and a bit like a package tour. As for outer space . . . well, some people say it's rather like Australia, and other people say it's more like measles."

Marmalade thought for a moment.

"Is there long division in space?" she asked.

"Oh, no, I shouldn't think so, dear."

"Are there nuns in space?"

"Not as far as my information goes."

"OK," said Marmalade. "I'll go."

Mr and Mrs Atkins were delighted.

"Well, er, when does it all, er . . . ?" said Mr Atkins.

"No time like the present!" said Mrs Allgood briskly. "Come in, boys!"

And to Marmalade's amazement, two enormous men in what looked like Babygro suits and moon boots, leapt in through the window. One of them had a moustache and looked rather like Sister Conception.

"This the client?" said one of them, grabbing Mr Atkins and dragging him to the door like a sack of potatoes.

"Help!" said Mr Atkins.

"No, no, Captain Conch!" shrilled Mrs Allgood. "The child!"

The other enormous man grabbed hold of Marmalade. She suddenly realised that she might have made a big mistake.

"Sign here," said Captain Conch to Mr Atkins.

"Here, hang on," yelled Marmalade. "I've changed me mind! Gerroff! I'm not going!"

But it was too late. Mr Atkins had signed the form.
"Bye, darling!" called Marmalade's mother cheerfully.
"Have a lovely time!" trilled Mrs Allgood.
Marmalade Atkins was bound for outer space.

Marmalade blasts off

"Call this a spaceship?" said Marmalade. "It's more like my dad's old Dormobile!"

It was indeed a very tatty old spaceship. Marmalade was sitting strapped tightly in a very uncomfortable seat with broken springs and the stuffing coming out. In front of her Colonel Perry was fiddling with a row of switches which kept falling off, and Captain Conch was reading a comic and eating apples. From somewhere below came a faint humming sound, and the whole place smelt like an old horsebox.

"Call this a spaceship?" she said again.

Colonel Perry turned round. He was a huge fat man with a sad face and steel-rimmed spectacles.

"Don't you be sarcastic about our gallant craft, Marmalade Atkins," he said. "It's penetrated more galaxies than you've had hot dinners."

Suddenly a shower of sparks hissed out of the control panel and lights flashed on and off. Captain Conch went into a panic.

"What's happening?" he yelled. "We're all going to die!"

"Oh, pull yourself together, Conch," grumbled Colonel Perry. "It's only the microwave oven again. No hot dinners on this trip. Malfunction in the Cottage Pie. Now please ensure your seat belts are securely fastened for take-off."

"What a farce," said Marmalade. "This thing'll never take off."

"Just you wait and see, cleverclogs," said Captain Conch crossly.

"What do you call this thing anyway?" said Marmalade.

"Pauline," said Conch rather shyly.

"*Pauline?*" said Marmalade, laughing a loud rude laugh. "What sort of name is *that* for a spaceship?"

"A very good name!" said Colonel Perry, sounding very hurt. "It happens to be my mother's name, if you want to know! Now, stand by for countdown!"

"Oh, come on," said Marmalade. "No one says that any more! You must be joking!"

"Five!" said Colonel Perry. "Four!"

"If you two are so clever. . . ." said Marmalade . . .

"Three!"

"Why are you still in Babygro suits?"

"Two!"

"One!"

The tatty old Space-Dormobile trembled and shook, and Captain Conch's Marmite sandwiches flew around the cockpit.

"Blast-off!" yelled Colonel Perry.

There was a huge roar, and to her amazement Marmalade felt herself pinned back in her seat. There was an enormous weight on her chest as if she was being sat on by seven donkeys. In front of her she could see the windscreen flapping like a sheet of cellophane, and Colonel Perry hanging on to the shuddering control lever.

Then everything went black.

Marmalade didn't know how long it was before she opened her eyes. When she did, she found to her surprise that she was still sitting in her tatty old seat. The Space-Dormobile still seemed to be in one piece. There was a faint humming sound and a few groans and rattles.

Ahead of her Captain Conch and Colonel Perry sat with their feet up on the control panel. Captain Conch was eating a banana and Colonel Perry was knitting. But the most amazing thing was that through the windscreen all that could be seen was . . . nothing. A whole lot of black nothing, with here and there faint bright pinpricks that just had to be stars. Marmalade rubbed her eyes and looked again. No mistake. They must really be in space!

There was a faint ping and Marmalade found that her

seat belt had freed itself. She could move! She scrambled out of her seat and went forward.

"All right," she said, "you've convinced me. We're in space. Now what?"

Colonel Perry turned round from his knitting.

"Nothing," he said.

"What d'you mean?" said Marmalade.

"Well, this is it," said Conch, pointing out into the blackness.

"But there's nothing there!" said Marmalade.

"Well, that's space for you," said Captain Conch.

"But I thought it was supposed to be dangerous, thrilling, and frightening!" said Marmalade, puzzled.

Colonel Perry laughed so much he dropped his knitting.

"Oh, dear, oh dear," he said.

"I've seen it on telly, cock, you can't fool me," said Marmalade.

But the astronauts were not impressed.

"Not dangerous and frightening?" said Marmalade in a small voice.

"Sorry," said the Colonel. "The thing about space, and the reason you have been sent here, is that it is very very boring."

"There's so much of it, you see," said Captain Conch gloomily.

"Well, I think that *you* are boring," said Marmalade rudely.

"Oh yes, we are," said Colonel Perry. "Very boring."

He sounded quite proud of it.

"Colonel Perry is the most boring astronaut in the whole Solar System," said Captain Conch, and Colonel Perry smiled modestly.

"I don't get this," said Marmalade.

"Oh dear," said Colonel Perry, "didn't you know? The whole point of Very Extreme Treatment is to Bore you into Being Good."

"But I can't stand being bored," said Marmalade. "I go berserk!"

"Well," said Colonel Perry. "Compared to a voyage in space with us, long division is almost unbearably thrilling."

"But . . . how long does the trip last?" asked Marmalade.

The astronauts grinned.

"For all eternity!"

Click click, click click went Colonel Perry's knitting needles. Chomp chomp, chomp chomp went Captain Conch on his Marmite sandwiches. And Marmalade felt herself becoming sleepier and sleepier as the fat little spacecraft bumbled slowly across the vast black nothingness of the universe.

Marmalade and the Lord of the Universe

Marmalade was awake again. The light was very dim, and somewhere she could hear a faint snoring. For a moment she thought she was back in her own bedroom at home, and the snoring was her dad, tired out with swindling people, poking pigs and jogging jogs.

But no. There was that faint humming; and now she could make out the dim shapes of the two gallant astronauts snoring away in their Babygro suits. She was still in the Space-Dormobile. Still lost in space, with no one to care where she was.

This wouldn't do. She was starting to feel sorry for herself. No good, that.

"Now's my chance to explore," she said to herself.

"Put meself about a bit, see what's what."

She unfastened her safety belt and fumbled her way to the back of the spacecraft, the part she hadn't been able to see before. With any luck, she would be able to find something useful. Superglue, itching powder, lifeboats, distress rockets, something, anyway.

But all she could find in the astronauts' cupboards were vast reserves of Marmite sandwiches and miles of pink and blue knitting wool. No good. Not even Superman could hatch an escape plan out of Marmite sandwiches and knitting wool. She would have to explore further.

Stumbling over a pile of Conch and Perry's books, (*Avoiding excitement on Mars and Venus, How to make sure nothing happens in Space, Ten great bores of the universe, Fifty ways of making people fed up with you*), Marmalade found herself standing in front of a little flickering screen labelled EARTHPROBE. It had two little knobs underneath it. Marmalade twiddled both of them, and the flickering screen cleared.

Marmalade found she was looking at an aerial view of the Convent of the Blessed Limit. She twiddled the right hand knob and found herself getting a closer and closer view . . . and there were Sister Conception and Sister Purification, clear as daylight, playing darts in their private office!

Marmalade twiddled the left hand knob . . . yes, now she could hear what they were saying!

"One hundred!" said Sister Purification, taking the darts out of the board. "At this rate we'll carry off the All Convents Darts Cup."

"Yeah. Great, sister," said Sister Conception. But she

looked depressed. Her moustache was drooping and the spring had gone out of her step. She threw the darts at the board and two of them fell out.

"Is something troubling you, sister?"

"It's . . . Marmalade Atkins," said Sister Conception.

"Somehow it's all too easy without her. I think of her out there, whirling round the vast and silent universe, and then I think of how I used to chase her round the dorm with a baseball bat, and oh, sister . . . I miss her, I miss her!"

And Sister Conception broke down into tears with her head in her great hairy hands.

"Don't you worry, cock!" shouted Marmalade, as the picture on the screen shrank to a tiny dot. "Don't you worry! I'll be back . . . somehow!"

"Well, would you believe it," she said to herself. "They miss me!"

Marmalade peered round. She was beginning to get used to the dim blue light of the sleeping spacecraft. It was strange: everything seemed familiar, like the battered old van in the yard at home, but there seemed to be much more space now.

She could see rows of cloudy glass panels stretching away from her all the way to the rear of the craft. Now what could they be for? Not more Marmite sandwiches, surely? She crept up to one of them and tried to peer through the glass. There seemed to be some sort of dim outline behind it. And then she saw a tiny metal knob at the side of the panel.

And, being Marmalade, she pressed it.

The panel slid back silently and Marmalade leapt back with a gasp of alarm. There behind the panel was a life-size doll of a sweetly-smiling little girl, with curly hair, pale waxy features, and horrid little white ankle socks. Or was it a doll?

"Aargh!" said Marmalade. "One of the Living Dead!"

"Hello," said the little girl, in a voice like Teeny Tiny Tears. "My name's Mandy. Who are you? Will you be my friend?"

"Certainly not!" said Marmalade, horrified, "What are you? How did you get like this?"

"Hello," said the creature again. "My name's Mandy. What's yours? I used to be bad, but now I'm good, and happy, too!
They washed the bad thoughts right out of my brain
And now I shall never be naughty again!"

Marmalade slammed the panel shut, and pressed the knob on the next panel. That one, too, slid back silently, and there was another of the Living Dead!

"Hello. My name's Candy? What's yours? Will you be my friend. I used to be—"

"Oh, no!" moaned Marmalade, and slammed that panel shut too.

How many more of them were there? How many girls had come to the Space-Dormobile as bad as Marmalade and had finished up like this? Worse still: was this what was going to happen to Marmalade?

"So that's what they want to do with me," she said aloud. "Well, I won't let them. Somehow, I have got to stay bad. Because if I'm not bad, I'm not me. Right?"

"Right," said a gloomy voice from the shadows at the back of the spacecraft.

Marmalade turned. On the shelf under the rear window was a dog. A nodding dog. A nodding bloodhound! For the first time since blast-off, Marmalade felt she had a friend on board.

"Talking to me, mate?" she said.   The nodding dog nodded. "Right," he said.

"Here," said Marmalade, "Nodding dogs nod, they don't talk."

"Now and then they do," said the nodding bloodhound. "When they feel like it. Actually I happen to be one of the Lords of the Universe."

"Oh, yeah?" said Marmalade. "Don't make me laugh! One of the Lords of the Universe a nodding bloodhound? Do me a favour, cock!"

"If I'm a Lord of the Universe I can appear in any form I choose, Marmalade Atkins. And I happen to like nodding dogs. All right?" The nodding bloodhound sounded quite offended.

"Yeah, all right," said Marmalade. "Well, look, what have you appeared *for*? I mean, I'm in bad trouble here. Are you going to help me out of it, or are you just going to lie there with your tongue hanging out?"

"Marmalade Atkins," said the bloodhound solemnly.

"You have stumbled on one of the great laws of existence. There are some people whose purpose in life is to muck about. You are one of them. To turn you into a goody would dangerously interfere with the laws of the Universe. You may not be nice, Marmalade Atkins, but you are necessary."

"Well, thanks a lot," said Marmalade. "Can we go home now then?"

"Not yet," said the nodding bloodhound. "First you must undergo the Ordeal of Excruciating Tedium, without your brains turning into sawdust."

"Why?" said Marmalade.

"So that you will have a chance of seizing the Golden Key for the Reverse Thrust System."

"Oh, blimey," said Marmalade. "Isn't there some easier way, like sticking everyone together with Superglue?"

"Unfortunately not."

"All right then, dogwog. Where's this key then?"

"On a chain round the neck of the Spacehols Fungirl. It is she who will give you the Ordeal of Excruciating Tedium. Do not underestimate her. People have been known to go mad with boredom when she's only telling them the time. She will probably take you to the Potman's Grotto. The ultimate test."

"How can I withstand it?" said Marmalade.

"Think about very interesting things," said the dog.

"You mean . . . like archbishops falling into giant vats of jelly?" asked Marmalade.

"That would do very well. And when she thinks you have gone into the Trance of the Living Dead, wait till you hear me bark twice."

"Then what?"

But the Lord of the Universe had had his say. He just nodded his gloomy old chops at her. Nod, nod. Nod, nod.

Marmalade and the Potman's Grotto

Next morning Colonel Perry and Captain Conch both seemed to be in a very good mood.

"What's up, cock?" said Marmalade.

"Oh, you're for it today, Marmalade Atkins," said the Colonel. "Potman's grotto, I shouldn't wonder. Beam in the Spacehols Fungirl!"

Captain Conch wiped a streak of Marmite off the Beam director and pressed the button. All the air in the Space-Dormobile seemed to shimmer and bend, and a human form solidified before their eyes.

Reeny the Spacehols Fungirl (for that was who it was) looked a little bit like Mrs Allgood (except that she had silver space boots and purple hair) and a little bit like Signora Nora from Eurohols.

"Hello, holidaymakers!" shrieked Reeny the Fungirl. "Where are all the Good Girls today?"

All the panels slid back, and all the poor brainwashed Good Girls chorused, "Here we are, Reeny!"

"Say bonjorno, Reeny!" said the Fungirl.

"Bonjorno, Reeny!" howled the Good Girls, Conch, and Perry.

"Bonjorno, girls, and bonjorno, boys, and a special bonjorno to our new friend Marmalade!" said Reeny.

"Huh," said Marmalade.

"That's the way, dear," said Reeny. "Well I'm sure we're all going to have a lovely time seeing all the sights etcetera. I know they're going to be very very lovely and typical etcetera, because today we're going to the very very lovely and popular Potman's Grotto!"

"Ooh!" trilled the Good Girls.

"Boo!" said Marmalade.

"Super!" said Reeny.

Marmalade felt as if she'd quite like to fall into a trance there and then. The bloodhound was right. This woman was very boring indeed!

"Now, Marmalade dear," said Reeny, "I'd like you to notice ahead of you a very very lovely and typical view of this part of the universe . . ."

"Nothing there at all," said Marmalade grumpily.

"That's right, dear, nothing there at all," said the Fungirl cheerfully, "and if you turned to the right or the left or turned back round on yourself you'd see just exactly the same, *nothing there at all*! Very very lovely, very characteristico etcetera . . . But now we are approaching the Grotto itself!"

"Ooh!" trilled the Good Girls.

"Boo!" said Marmalade.

"Soooper!" said the Fungirl.

Marmalade turned round and saw an extraordinary sight. Floating freely in the blackness of space, with nothing you could see to support it, was a large flat splodge of green muck, about the size of a school playground. In the middle of the splodge of green muck was a sort of slimy lake, with a cave in the middle of it. At the entrance to the cave was a huge stone table rather like a huge and poisonous toadstool, covered with warty lumps. And sitting at the table was the Potman. The Potman was green and slimy, like his lake, and covered in warty lumps, like his table. He was the most disgusting looking creature Marmalade had ever seen. In a curious way he also reminded her of her dad.

"There he is!" shrieked Reeny. "Pepe the Potman! Say Bonjorno, Pepe!"

"Bonjorno, Pepe!" said the Good Girls.

"Bonjorno, Pepe!" said Captain Conch and Colonel Perry.

"Morning, cock," said Marmalade.

The Potman turned his head and stared blearily in their direction, and raised his warty green arm in a clumsy salute.

"Ar," he said.

He *is* just like my dad, thought Marmalade.

"He's just like my dad," said Marmalade.

"No he's not," said Reeny crossly. "He's much more

primitive and genuine."

"And lovely, etcetera," said Marmalade.

"That's right, dear," said Reeny. "Now for a lovely treat. Pepe the Potman is going to make us a pot I think, a pot, just for us, with typical decoration etcetera, very very lovely and characteristico!"

"Get on with it then," said Marmalade.

"Very very slowly, the Potman groped around his table with his green and warty arm until his fat green fingers closed around one of the huge slimy-looking pots by his side. His brow furrowed in a frown. He stared at the pot as if he had never seen a pot before in his life. (Very like my dad, thought Marmalade). Then the Potman slowly raised the pot above his head with both hands, and brought it down sharply on the table.

Smash! Pieces of broken pot flew all over the grotto.

"Ooooh!" chorused the Good Girls.

"Sooper!" said Reeny the Fungirl.

"Ungh," said Pepe the Potman, staring at the broken pieces in a baffled way.

"Here," said Marmalade. "That's not making pots, that's smashing them. Barmy!"

"Don't upset the Potman, dear," said Reeny the Fungirl. "He didn't make one that time, but this time I'm sure he's going to do something very very lovely!"

Slowly the Potman groped around in the pile of pots by his side, until he held another in his fist. Slowly he stared at it as if he had never seen a pot before. And slowly he lifted it above his head with both hands, paused, and brought it sharply down on the table.

"Smash!

"Oooh!"

"Sooper!"

"Ungh!"

"Here, cock, you're barmy!"

"Don't upset the Potman, dear, he didn't make one that time, but this time I'm sure he's going to do something very very lovely!"

Slowly the Potman groped around in the pile of pots by his side, until he held another in his fist . . . And then Marmalade realised what it was all about. This was the Ordeal of Excruciating Tedium. She was going to have to watch poor old Pepe the Potman smash pot after pot until her brains turned to sawdust. What a horrible way to go! She was going to have to think very hard indeed about Archbishops falling in jelly, or she'd finish up like the Good Girls.

She imagined an immensely fat Archbishop in a long red robe and a huge gold hat inspecting an enormous jelly factory.

"Life, indeed, is very like a bowl of jelly," he was saying.

"Watch out for that vat, Your Grace!"

Splash!

"Oooh!"

"Soooper!"

"Ungh!"

Slowly the Potman groped around in the pile of pots
. . . No, I can't take the risk. Even to read about the Ordeal
of Excruciating Tedium will put you in severe danger of
Sawdust Brain. The only way to stand up to it is to imagine
very interesting things, and if you start thinking about very
interesting things you will stop reading this book, which
would be a pity as we are very near the end now and you
might as well hang on and see what happens. So I think the
best thing to do is to skip the next seven hours at the
Potman's Grotto.

Seven hours later, the pile of broken pots on Pepe the
Potman's table was ten feet high, and Marmalade Atkins
was running out of Archbishops. Her eyelids were
drooping. She was beginning to slump in her chair. And
Reeny the Spacehols Fungirl had the beginnings of a
triumphant smile on her face.

Smash!

"Oooh!"

"Soooper!"

"Ungh!"

"Well he didn't make one that time, but this time . . .
I'm sure . . ." Reeny's voice was slow and soothing as she
crept closer and closer to Marmalade's chair. "This time
. . . I'm sure . . . he's going to do . . . yes, I think she's
gone at last. Marmalade's brains have turned to sawdust!"

They nearly had, too. Marmalade felt as if she was
swimming through a lake of treacle. But then faint and far

away, she heard two gruff barks. The nodding bloodhound!

She forced her eyes open, and saw that the startled Fungirl was leaning right over her, and the little Golden Key was dangling on a string right in front of her eyes.

"Archbishops in jelly!" yelled Marmalade, and yanked the key off the string.

"Not the Reverse Thrust System!" screamed Reeny the Fungirl. "You don't know what you're doing!"

But Marmalade had already leapt past her, and was diving for the control panel. There was a little slot marked RTS in the middle of the panel, and Marmalade plunged straight for it. Conch and Perry both dived for her at the same moment, but missed and went rolling over and over each other to the back of the Dormobile.

The key was in!

There was a second of complete silence and stillness, then the spacecraft started to whirl round and round on its axis as though it was trying to disappear up its own exhaust pipe. Faster and faster it went with a noise like forty fairground rides gone mad, and Marmalade saw Captain Conch, Colonel Perry, Reeny the Fungirl, and all the Living Dead whirling round and round in a crazy technicolour blur. Then everything went black.

Marmalade opened her eyes. She was in bed, she was not dead, and as far as she could tell her brains had not turned to sawdust. The sun was streaming through her bedroom

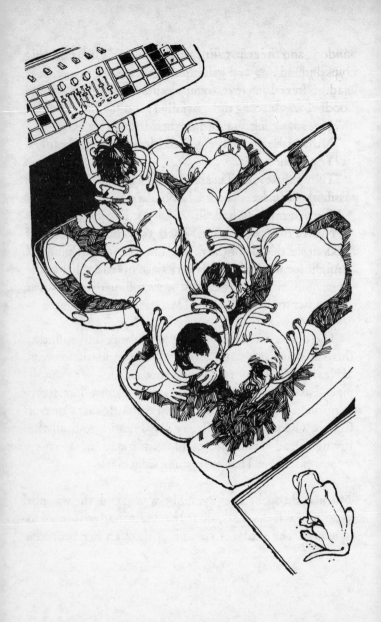

window, and from the paddock she could hear Torchy and Gypsy whinnying and galumphing about. She turned her head. There on the windowsill sat the nodding bloodhound, nodding thoughtfully away.

"Morning, cock," said Marmalade.

"Marmalade!" yelled her mother from downstairs.

"Yes, cock?"

"Time to get ready for school! And Marmalade, do you possibly thing you could try to be good today?"

Marmalade grinned.

"Not my job, that, is it?" she said to the nodding bloodhound.

And the nodding bloodhound shook his head.

MARMALADE ATKINS' DREADFUL DEEDS

If you think this is going to be one of those books in which the bad girl learns her lesson and becomes good and nice for ever, you are wrong!

When Marmalade Atkins feels like doing a bad thing she does it, which is why everyone says she's the worst girl in the world. No one likes her – no one except Rufus the diabolical talking donkey. He likes Marmalade's style. Together they start putting themselves about – as the star turn in the El Poko Nightclub. And that's only the beginning. Look out world! Marmalade Atkins is about to have one amazingly good time.

The first hilarious adventure featuring the world's most horrible heroine.

ON THE EDGE
Gillian Cross

A brilliant thriller by the award-winning author of *Wolf* and *The Great Elephant Chase*.

Tug pushed the door as far open as he could. Squatting down, he peered through the narrow crack and saw what was hanging outside, across the opening. A heavy padlock, snapped shut.

That was when he realized it *wasn't* all a mistake. He must have been kidnapped by the strange man and woman who'd brought him to this remote Derbyshire cottage. But he couldn't remember how it had happened, and the things the couple were saying just didn't make sense. If only they'd stop playing that endless, deafening brass-band music . . .

On the Edge is a fascinating, unputdownable thriller that is simply brimming with suspense.

YOUR MOTHER WAS A NEANDERTHAL
Jon Scieszka

The dinosaur looked at us and roared again. We went to the Stone Age to become kings, and were about to become lunch.

What better way to avoid doing maths homework than to take a trip (with the help of Joe's magic book) back to the Stone Age. The Time Warp Trio plan to wow their ancestors with modern inventions, like juggling balls, water pistols and Walkmans. But dinosaurs, dangerous cavewomen, tigers, earthquakes and woolly mammoths are just a few of their problems.

'You say there is nothing for boys to read? Can't find anything that mixes adventure, comedy and a tad of hocus-pocus? Never fear, the Time Warp Trio has arrived' – *Booklist*

THE BFG
Roald Dahl

Just imagine suddenly knowing you may be eaten for breakfast in the very near future; dropped like a rasher of bacon into a frying pan sizzling with fat.

This is exactly what worries Sophie when she is snatched from her bed in the middle of the night by a giant with a stride as long as a tennis court. Luckily for Sophie, the BFG is far more jumble than his disgusting neighbours, whose favourite pastime is guzzling and swallomping nice little chidders. Sophie is determined to stop all this and so she and the BFG cook up an ingenious plan to rid the world of troggle-humping, bogthumping giants for ever!

CALAMITY WITH THE FIEND
Sheila Lavelle

Charlie's best friend Angela is more like a best FIEND!

With Angela around Charlie always finds herself in a whole heap of trouble. Whether it's a plan to kidnap a dog and then collect the reward, or claim first prize in a painting competition, Charlie finds herself up to her ears in one hilarious calamity after another.

RAMONA THE GREAT
Beverly Cleary

'Growing up is hard work,' said Mr Quimby ... 'Sometimes being grownup is hard work.'

The arrival of Howie Kemp's rich Uncle Hobart from Saudi Arabia heralds a sequence of unexpected events in the Quimby household. For Ramona, there are exciting times like being a bridesmaid; worrying times like maybe having to move if Mr Quimby gets a new job; and sad times like when Picky-Picky dies. But Ramona survives all these ups and downs, proving that she is winning at growing up and that she is still the same old wonderful, blunderful Ramona!

A HANDFUL OF THIEVES
Nina Bawden

Set a thief to catch a thief!

There were five of them – which is why they were called a handful of thieves. Not that they were real thieves, of course. They just had to act like thieves to catch the sinister Mr Gribble.

He pretended to be just an ordinary lodger, but Sid knew better. Apart from anything else, it wasn't right for a tall, thin man like him to talk with a voice like that!

So when Gribble scarpered with Gran's savings, Sid wasn't surprised. But he was determined to get the money back – even if it did mean the five children had to behave themselves!